New Paige Press, LLC
NewPaigePress.com

New Paige Press and the distinctive ladybug icon are registered trademarks of New Paige Press, LLC

Text and illustration copyright by the REED Foundation for Autism
First edition

All rights reserved. No part of this publication, or the characters within it, may be reproduced or distributed in any form or by any means without prior written consent from the publisher.

ISBN 978-1-7345980-1-8

Printed and bound in China

New Paige Press provides special discounts when purchased in larger volumes for premiums and promotional purposes, as well as for fundraising and educational use. Custom editions can also be created for special purposes. In addition, supplemental teaching material can be provided upon request. For more information, please visit reedfoundationforautism.org/onebigcanvas.

The Molding of Clay

WRITTEN BY
Mr. Jay

PAINTED BY
Luis Peres

It was just before noon on a bright, sunny day, and the paintbrushes felt too excited to play.

A short bit ago, near their grand masterpiece,
the brushes were gathered by a paintbrush named Reese,
who happily told them, "Our artistic friend Clay
will be coming to visit us later today.
Let's get ourselves ready, let's all do our best,
let's do something special to welcome our guest."

The studio buzzed and felt quite alive
with news that a new friend soon would arrive.

They found a blank banner,
and some pieces of twine,
that they used to create
a huge Welcome! sign.
Then they got some nice paint,
and in two or three hours
they painted their friend
a bouquet of bright flowers.

And just as they ran out of yellow and blue,
they heard a voice shout,
"HEY BRUSHES! GUESS WHO?"
The brushes all turned to see their friend Clay -
lumpy and bumpy, mushy and grey.
A jovial fellow, always in a good mood,
he shouted,
"I'M STARVED! LET'S GET US SOME FOOD!"

But all of a sudden, a paintbrush named Paul
laid down on the ground, and curled into a ball.
He covered his ears, and squinted his eyes,
while Clay kept on shouting,

"WELL, THAT'S A SURPRISE! WHAT'S WRONG WITH HIM?"

he asked the brush crowd,
while Paul kept repeating, "It's too loud, it's too loud."

"Loud sounds bother him," Reese said. "So you know... sometimes when we speak, we try to speak low."

Just then a small brush
came with canvas in hand
and showed it to Clay,
"Look! Isn't this grand?
I painted a boat,
with a sail and a mast,
It's out in the ocean,
and it's sailing real fast.

"Boats are the best,
with their captains and crews,
sailboats and whaleboats
and yachts and canoes."

For the next several minutes, that small brush named Jerry told Clay all about the Long Island Ferry, and the cruise ship Titanic and how it was made, when it was launched and how much it weighed.

Clay interrupted,
"THAT'S ALL VERY NICE,
BUT YOU'VE TOLD ME THESE FACTS, AND YOU'VE TOLD ME THEM TWICE!"
Reese said, "Boats are his thing, it's what he loves most,
whether out on the waves, or docked 'long the coast.
Some brushes are different, so we like to remind,
It's kind to be caring, so take care to be kind."

Clay thought it over, then smiled really wide,
and kept his voice low as he kindly replied,
"AS CLAY I CAN MOLD MYSELF INTO NEW THINGS,
LIKE RACE CARS OR SPACE STARS OR HORSES WITH WINGS.
I'LL BE BACK IN A MOMENT!"
and Clay rolled away -
the brushes were stunned, with nothing to say.

Clay finally came back,
but in the shape of a ship,
to take his friend Jerry
on a fun, pretend trip.
"And Paul, don't you worry,
we'll just quietly float,
on painted blue waves,
to our nautical note."

Meet the Cast of The Molding of Clay

Kelli Fowler, MA, BCBA

Kelli Fowler is a Board Certified Behavior Analyst (BCBA) who holds a Master of Arts in special education and is a certified general and special education teacher. She has been educating children on the autism spectrum since 2004. As the clinical director at REED Academy, Kelli focuses on educational services, behavior, and transition supports. She also works with school districts and other organizations to bring awareness to autism and integrate education into the community.

Joseph Novak, EdD, BCBA-D, CCC-SLP, ATP

Joe Novak is a Board Certified Behavior Analyst-Doctoral Level (BCBA-D) who holds a Doctorate of Education in special education and is an ASHA-certified speech and language pathologist. He is also an adjunct professor at Kean University. As the director of curriculum & technology at REED Academy, Joe oversees speech and language, augmentative communication, curriculum development, and technology initiatives.

Mr. Jay, Author

Mr. Jay is a reformed business author who has turned his attention to the far more creative, exciting, and competitive world of children's picture books. His titles include *Ricky, the Rock that Couldn't Roll*, *The Bear and the Fern*, *The Masteroiece* and others.

He credits his daughter, Bria, for inspiring many of his story ideas, and his fiancé, Amanda, for pointing out how to make each book a whole lot better. He can be reached at www.MeetMrJay.com.

Luis Peres, Artist/Illustrator

Born in the south of Portugal, Luis has been illustrating professionaly since 1992. His work includes children's books, book covers, short stories, postcards, and board games. He also illustrates regularly for publishing companies specializing in school books. Luis is happiest when illustrating imaginary worlds, whimsical characters, or anything related to fantasy and sci-fi landscapes.

Luis' work can be viewed at www.icreateworlds.com.

An initiative of the REED Foundation for Autism, the "One Big Canvas" series seeks to celebrate differences, showcasing how each individual, regardless of his or her own unique qualities, can be an integral part of a much larger picture. Autism is a highly prevalent and often misunderstood neurological disability. Our hope is that these positive and engaging children's stories will promote acceptance, understanding, and kindness for all. To learn more about Autism Spectrum Disorder, please visit reedfoundationforautism.org.

"The Molding of Clay" is made possible in part by a grant from the Columbia Bank Foundation.

Columbia Bank

The "One Big Canvas" series is funded in part through a grant from the Special Child Health and Autism Registry, New Jersey Department of Health.
REED Foundation for Autism is a 501(c)(3)